Be Brave, Willa Bean!

To Maddie!

·2022

Be Brave,
Willa Beard

To Maddie!

Be Brave, Willa Bean!

by Cecilia Galante
illustrated by Kristi Valiant

A STEPPING STONE BOOK™
Random House   New York

For Joseph, my sweetest boy —C.G.

For my Jovie, may you be full of joy and
not fear the dark (Psalm 23) —K.V.

This is a work of fiction. Names, characters, places, and incidents either are the
product of the author's imagination or are used fictitiously. Any resemblance to
actual persons, living or dead, events, or locales is entirely coincidental.

Text copyright © 2011 by Cecilia Galante
Cover art and interior illustrations copyright © 2011 by Kristi Valiant

Published in the United States by Random House Children's Books, a division of
Random House, Inc., New York.

Random House and the colophon are registered trademarks and A Stepping Stone
Book and the colophon are trademarks of Random House, Inc.

Visit us on the Web!
SteppingStonesBooks.com
randomhouse.com/kids

Educators and librarians, for a variety of teaching tools, visit us at
randomhouse.com/teachers

Library of Congress Cataloging-in-Publication Data
Galante, Cecilia.
Be brave, Willa Bean! / by Cecilia Galante ; illustrated by Kristi Valiant.
p. cm. — (Little wings ; #2)
"A Stepping Stone book."
Summary: Cupid Willa Bean does not want to admit that she does not like
flying high, or in the dark, but during a sleepover, she has to face her fears.
ISBN 978-0-375-86948-8 (pbk.) — ISBN 978-0-375-96948-5 (lib. bdg.) —
ISBN 978-0-375-98353-5 (ebook)
[1. Fear—Fiction. 2. Fear of the dark—Fiction. 3. Sleepovers—Fiction.
4. Cupid (Roman deity)—Fiction.] I. Valiant, Kristi, ill. II. Title.
PZ7.G12965 Be 2011 [Fic]—dc22   2011007276

Printed in the United States of America

Contents

Willa Bean's World

Willa Bean Skylight is a cupid. Cupids live in a faraway place called Nimbus, which sits just alongside the North Star, in a tiny pocket of the Milky Way. Nimbus is made up of three white stars and nine clouds, all connected by feather bridges. It has a Cupid Academy, where cupids go to school, a garden cloud, where they grow and store their food, and lots and lots of playgrounds.

Willa Bean lives on Cloud Four with her mother and father, her big sister, Ariel, and her baby brother, Louie. Cloud Four is soft and green. The air around it smells like rain and pineapples. Best of all, Willa Bean's best friend, Harper, also lives on Cloud Four, just a few cloudbumps away.

When cupids are ready, they are given special Earth tasks. That means they have to fly down to Earth to help someone who is having a hard time. Big cupids, like Willa Bean's parents, help Earth grown-ups with things like falling in love. Little cupids, like Willa Bean, help Earth kids if they feel mad, sad, or just plain stuck. Working with Earth people is the most important job a cupid has. It can be hard work, too, but there's nothing that Willa Bean would rather do.

Are you ready for a peek into Willa Bean's world? It's just a few cloudbumps away, so let's go!

Chapter 1

Sleepover!

Willa Bean bounced out of bed. Today was Thunderday! That meant that there was only one more day of school until the weekend. On weekends, Willa Bean went treasure hunting with her best friend, Harper. Afterward, they flew all over Nimbus, looking for fun things to do. Weekends were the best!

Willa Bean got dressed in her school uniform with the red stripe on the bottom. She brushed her purple wings with

1

the silver tips until they were soft and fluffy. Then she gave them a little pep talk.

"Good morning, little wings!" she said. "You look absolutely wonderful today!"

Her wings fluttered with excitement. They loved Willa Bean just as much as she loved them. A few weeks ago, Willa Bean had finally learned how to use her wings. Now she could fly, like all the rest of the cupids. This meant that she could play flying games at recess instead of sitting on the swings. And she could fly to Cloud Five with Harper when they wanted to visit their treasure chest.

Willa Bean was very happy that she could fly. She liked to make sure that her wings stayed happy, too.

Next, Willa Bean brushed her hair. She brushed and brushed, exactly the way Mama told her to do. Then she tried to mash it down on the sides so that it was not so wide. She used both hands. She pressed down very hard. But every time Willa Bean lifted her hands, her hair boinged back out again.

Willa Bean scrunched her nose. She shook her head. She even took out the three copper coins she had hidden inside a very tight curl, and put them in her soft leather pouch instead. Then she tried to mash her hair down again.

BOING!

Willa Bean sighed. It was hopeless. Her hair would not behave. Oh well. Mama was just going to have to live with it for one more day.

"Bonjour!" A voice floated in from the window.

Willa Bean turned around. "Hi there, Snooze!" She gave her brown owl an eyelash kiss and patted his head. "How was Paris?"

"Actually," Snooze said, "I went further than Paris last night."

"Where did you go?" Willa Bean asked.

"Morocco," Snooze answered. "It's a marvelous place. And I have some family there. We had a sensational time together."

"Where's Morocco?" asked Willa Bean.

"In Africa." Snooze flapped his wings. He got excited when he talked about his travels. "It's very hot and dry, even at night. And it's full of wonderful smells. Spicy smells that make your feathers curl!"

Willa Bean wrinkled her nose. "I don't like spicy too much," she said. "It makes my tongue feel tingly."

"To each his own." Snooze opened his beak and let out a yawn. "Well, I'm completely worn out," he said. "I'll see you

later, Willa Bean. Have a good day at school." Snooze slipped inside Willa Bean's closet. He settled himself in the corner and tucked his head under one wing. Then he closed his eyes.

"Sleep tight, Snooze," Willa Bean whispered. She pulled on her sandals and went downstairs.

Baby Louie was sitting in his high chair. He was wearing a diaper. Nothing else. There were Babyflakes in his hair. There were Babyflakes on his stomach. There were even Babyflakes in his ears! Baby Louie was not the neatest cupid in the world. In fact, he was somewhat of a slob. But Willa Bean loved him anyway.

Mama and Ariel were sitting at the table, eating breakfast.

"Everyone will get here at five," Ariel said to Mama. "And then we'll go up to my room and decide what we want to do for the rest of the night." Willa Bean slid into the chair next to her big sister. "And, Mama, please keep Willa Bean away from us." Ariel frowned at Willa Bean. "I don't want her hanging around during my sleepover. It will ruin everything."

"Sleepover?" Willa Bean sat up straight in her chair. Her curls *boing-boing*ed on top of her head. "Who's having a sleepover?"

"I am." Ariel pointed to herself. "Tomorrow night. And you're not invited."

"Mama!" Willa Bean cried. "If Ariel gets to have a sleepover, then I get to have one, too!"

"Another time." Mama raised an eyebrow. "You're not leaving this cloud until you brush that hair, Willa Bean."

"I already did!" Willa Bean said. "And I smooshed it, too! With both hands! Just like you said!"

Baby Louie threw a Babyflake on the floor. "Smooshie-gooshie!" he said.

"No throwing food," Mama said, looking sternly at Baby Louie.

"Smooshie!" Baby Louie said again.

Ariel rolled her eyes. She shook her head at Baby Louie and wrinkled her nose. Ariel did not have much patience for babies.

"It's not *fair*!" Willa Bean wailed. "Ariel gets to have all her cupids over tomorrow, and I'll be alone!"

"Gee whizzle, Willa Bean," Ariel said. "Sometimes I wonder if you should just stay home with Baby Louie. All you do is whine."

"You be quiet!" Willa Bean said.

Ariel made a googly face at Willa Bean. *"Baby,"* she said.

"Meany-pants!" Willa Bean yelled.

Baby Louie kicked the bottom of his high chair. "Gooshie!"

"That's enough, girls." Mama rubbed her forehead. "All right, Willa Bean," she said. "You may ask Harper to spend the night tomorrow. But Harper *only*. No one else."

"But, Mama!" Ariel started.

Mama raised a finger. "I will make *sure* they stay out of your way, Ariel. No one is going to wreck your slumber party. I promise." She turned and looked directly at Willa Bean. "And you have to help me keep that promise, Willa Bean. There is to be no bothering your big sister while Harper is here."

"NO MATTER WHAT," Ariel said, leaning in close to Willa Bean. "OR ELSE HARPER GOES HOME."

"Don't worry," Willa Bean said, taking a bite of her Wingfastic cereal. "I don't want to be part of your smelly old sleepover anyway. Harper and I will have our own fun."

And it was true, she thought.

If there was anyone in the universe who was more fun than her best friend, Harper, Willa Bean didn't know who it was.

They would have the best time ever.

Chapter 2

Making Plans

Just this past summer, Willa Bean had slept over at Harper's house. First, they went to Cloud Five, where their treasure chest was buried. They stayed there for a long time and looked at all their treasure. Then they put everything back and went to Harper's house for dinner. After that, they stayed up late, trying to count the stars outside the window. It took them a long, long time. They played with Harper's flying friend, Octavius, and practiced hanging upside down. Octavius was a bat. He was very good at hanging upside down. They told ghost stories and built a giant fort. It was the best sleepover in the whole world!

But Harper had never slept over at Willa Bean's house. Not even once.

Tomorrow was going to be the first time *Willa Bean* had a real sleepover! At her house!

Willa Bean jiggled and wiggled as she waited for the cloudbus. She could not wait to tell Harper the good news.

After a while, the cloudbus rumbled up. Mr. Bibby, who was the cloudbus driver, opened the door and let Willa Bean in. Mr. Bibby liked to wear bow ties. Today, he was wearing a blue bow tie with gold dots. "Good morning, Willa Bean!" he said.

"Hi, Mr. Bibby!" said Willa Bean. "I like your bow tie!"

"Thank you," Mr. Bibby said. "It's one of my favorites." He shut the door behind Willa Bean. "Take your seat now. And fasten your cloudbelt."

"Hey, Willa Bean!" Harper yelled. "I'm over here!"

Willa Bean ran down the middle of the cloudbus and sat in their favorite seat. "Guess what?" she asked.

Harper was eating a Snoogy Bar. She was making a big mess. It was a blueberry one with vanilla star sprinkles on top. "You found a treasure?" Harper asked.

"Nope! Guess again!"

Harper licked her fingers. The gooey blueberry mess smeared even more. "You flew to Paris with Snooze last night?"

"Nope, nope, nope-ity, nope!" Willa Bean wiggled her legs. "And Snooze didn't even go to Paris. He went to Morocco instead. They like spicy things there."

Harper popped the rest of the Snoogy Bar into her mouth and wiped her fingers on the seat. It made a sticky,

14

disgusting mess. She peeked over the seat at Mr. Bibby. He didn't notice. "Let's not sit in this seat on the way home," Harper said quietly.

Willa Bean yanked on Harper's sleeve. "Guess! Guess again!"

"I don't know, Willa Bean," Harper said. "I just guessed everything I could think of."

"Mama said you could sleep over!" Willa Bean hollered. "TOMORROW NIGHT! At our house!"

Harper fluffed her wings. "Wizzle-dizzle-doodad!" she yelled. "Really?"

"Really!" Willa Bean hopped up and down in her seat. "We can make Snoogy Bars, and stay up late, and build forts, and play with Snooze before he leaves for the night!"

"And we can have pillow fights and play

dress-up!" Harper bounced up and down in the seat. "And now that you know how to fly, we can go flying in the dark!"

Willa Bean stopped wiggling. "Fly in the dark?" she repeated.

"Yeah!" Harper yelled. "It's so fun! Last weekend, my dad took me flying around the back of the Milky Way. It took so long that by the time we turned around, it was almost midnight! It was so dark that I couldn't even see my hand in front of my face! It was awesome!"

Willa Bean swallowed. She had two night-lights in her room that Mama turned on every night before she went to sleep. And she liked having her door open a little so that the hall light could shine in. She did not like to sleep in the dark.

And she could not imagine *flying* in the dark.

It sounded much, much too scary.

"Oh, I don't think we'll have time to do anything like that," Willa Bean said.

"Why not?" Harper asked.

Willa Bean leaned in close to Harper's ear and covered her mouth with her hand. "Because Ariel's having a sleepover with all her cupid friends! So we have to figure out how we can play tricks on them!"

Harper's eyes were as round as golf balls behind her blue polka-dotted glasses. "Golly-wolly-wing-wang, Willa Bean! This is gonna be the best sleepover ever!"

"I know!" Willa Bean said. "It's gonna be the best sleepover in the whole uvinerse!"

Chapter 3

Tip-Top

Recess was Willa Bean's favorite part of school. It was even more fun since she had learned how to fly. Now she didn't have to sit on the swings by herself. Or stand and watch as everyone else played flying games.

Today, she joined the other cupids as they got in a big circle. They were going to play Wing Touch. But first, they had to decide who should be captain.

Wing Touch was one of Willa Bean's

favorite games. To play well, you had to fly very, very fast. Willa Bean loved flying fast. She was good at it. She couldn't wait to start playing.

"I want to be captain!" Vivi said. "Sophie got to be captain yesterday, so it's my turn!"

Vivi sat in front of Willa Bean in Class A. She had long red hair and tattled to Miss Twizzle if Willa Bean did anything wrong. Willa Bean was not one of Vivi's biggest fans. Not even a little bit.

"But you were captain on Moonday," Harper said to Vivi. "You can't be captain two times in the same week. It's Lola's turn!"

"Yeah!" said Raymond. "It *is* Lola's turn!"

"That's not fair!" Vivi's face turned pink. She stamped her foot. "We only had

a half recess on Moonday because of bow-
and-arrow practice! So I get to be captain
again!"

"No way!" Willa Bean said.

"Yes way!" shouted Vivi.

"Cupids!" Miss Twizzle hurried over. "Why don't you play a different game today? Something that doesn't involve captains?"

"I know!" Raymond jumped up and down behind Pedro. His little white wings wiggled excitedly. "I know, Miss Twizzle! We can play Tip-Top!"

There was a shout from the rest of the cupids. "Yeah! Let's play Tip-Top! Let's play Tip-Top!"

Everyone jumped up and down and yelled and clapped their hands.

Everyone except Willa Bean.

The Tip-Top game was a lot different from Wing Touch. In Tip-Top, each cupid tried to fly to the very tip-top of one of the baby clouds above them. If they reached it, they had to grab a piece of the cloud and bring it back down. Baby clouds were not one of the nine special clouds of Nimbus. They were too small. And too soft. But they were very, very high up. Willa Bean was sure they were at least a million-bajillion miles above them.

Only one thing scared Willa Bean more than the dark. And that was being up high. Being too high made her nervous. Maybe even a little bit more than nervous. What if her wings got tired while she was all the way up there? What if they pooped out? And what if she fell? *Then* what?

Willa Bean took a step back as the other cupids jumped up and down. She twisted a curl around one of her fingers and stayed very quiet.

"I want to go first!" Vivi said. She waved her arms. The big green bow in her hair flopped up and down. "Me, me, me, me!"

"You always get to go first," Hannah

said. "For everything. It's not fair."

Hannah was the tallest cupid in the whole class. She almost reached the top of Miss Twizzle's waist! Willa Bean wondered if Hannah ever got scared being so high up.

"It is *too* fair." Vivi smoothed her hair down with her fingers. "Besides, I'm the oldest. And so that's just the way it is."

"Let's pick a feather for it," Raymond suggested.

Raymond always had good ideas.

All the cupids reached over their shoulders and plucked a feather out of their wings. Willa Bean felt around until she found the tiniest feather she could find. She squished her face as she pulled it out. It hurt a little bit. Then she held it out in the middle of the circle along with everyone else.

Raymond looked at everyone's feather. "Sophie wins!" he shouted. "She has the longest feather! She gets to go first!"

Sophie clapped her hands. "Yay!" she yelled. Sophie was the littlest cupid in Class A, but she was very brave. She was always the first one to go down the highest slide in the playground. And she never even screamed.

Vivi stamped her foot. She tossed her hair and puffed out her bottom lip.

Willa Bean put the tiny feather back inside her wing. The jiggly-wiggly feeling inside her stomach was making her nervous. She wondered if there was a secret to flying high that she did not know about yet.

All the other cupids gathered around Sophie. She was getting ready to shoot up toward a baby cloud.

24

"Bend your knees real low," Harper suggested. "That always helps me go extra high."

"And keep your arms super-close to your ears," said Pedro.

"And point your fingers," said Raymond.

"And don't arch your back," said Lola.

"STOP!" Sophie clamped her hands over her ears. "I NEED SUPER-EXTRA QUIET WHEN I FLY!"

Willa Bean wondered if being quiet was the secret to flying high. She didn't know if she could be that quiet. Especially before she flew. Being quiet was too hard. At any time.

"Shhhh!" Pedro said. "Everyone stop talking!"

All the cupids fell silent.

Willa Bean watched Sophie carefully as

she stood in the middle of the circle.

Sophie took a deep breath. She bent her knees. She straightened her back. She raised her arms, pointed her fingers, and wiggled her wings.

And then she shot into the air, straight as a line.

Willa Bean looked up. All she could see were the bottoms of Sophie's brown school shoes. They were a little dirty. Something was stuck to one of the heels.

Slowly, Sophie stopped going up. Her shoes started coming back down. Willa Bean could see her socks, and her legs, and finally her wings. Sophie fluttered down next to her.

"I couldn't reach it!" Sophie gasped. "I tried and tried, but it's *so* high!"

Willa Bean shivered a little.

Harper patted Sophie on the back. "Ringle-dingle-doo-dah, Sophie! That was great! You were so close!"

Raymond, who was wearing a bright red hat today, was next.

"You should take off your hat," Hannah suggested. "That way, you'll go faster."

But Raymond did not take off his hat.

He said it was a lucky hat. Willa Bean wondered if Raymond's lucky hat was his secret to going up high. She did not have a lucky hat. Maybe it was time to get one.

Raymond bent his knees and straightened his back. He placed his arms close to his ears, just like Sophie. But when he went up in the air, he wobbled. And when he tried to straighten himself out, he wobbled again.

Down, down, down he came. His red hat was puffed wide with air. So were his cheeks.

"I *told* you to take off your hat!" Hannah insisted.

"It wasn't my hat!" Raymond said. "I've been feeling a little wobbly all day. Ever since this morning, actually. I don't think I ate enough breakfast."

Hannah rolled her eyes.

"Okay, now me!" Vivi pushed her way into the middle of the circle. She straightened her green bow and flattened her skirt. She closed her eyes and raised her arms above her head. She shot up into the air.

Vivi went very, very high. Even higher than Sophie. But she did not touch the baby cloud.

Vivi came back down. Her face was mad-looking. "I want another turn," she said. "My foot slipped when I tried to start! That's why I didn't get very high."

"No way!" Pedro said. "Harper and Lola and Hannah and Willa Bean all still have to go! There won't be time if you take another turn!"

"Hmph!" Vivi said.

Willa Bean took another tiny step outside the circle. She hoped no one noticed.

Hannah and Lola and Harper all had

their turns. Lola and Hannah went very high. Even higher than Vivi had gone. But they did not reach the tip-top of the baby cloud above them.

Harper took off from the ground like a rocket. She went so high that Willa Bean couldn't even see her shoes anymore.

"Wow!" Lola shouted. "Harper's *outta* here!"

The cupids put their hands over their eyes and squinted up into the sky.

"Do you think she got Tip-Top?" Pedro asked.

"*Maybe!*" Hannah yelled.

Suddenly, the bottom of Harper's shoes appeared. Then her socks, and her knees, and finally, all the rest of her. Harper stood back down on the ground. There was a big smile on her face. She opened her hand very slowly. Inside was a piece of baby

cloud. It was blue and fluffy and already starting to melt.

All the cupids yelled and jumped and patted Harper on the back. "Awesome, Harper! You did it! You did it!"

"Okay, Willa Bean!" Pedro shouted. "It's your turn! You're the last one! See if you can beat Harper!"

Willa Bean's stomach felt like it was full of fireflies. And they were whizzing around like crazy. She felt very horrible. And sick, too. Like she might throw up.

"Let's go, Willa Bean!" Harper shouted. "You can do it! Show us your stuff!"

Willa Bean swallowed hard. She walked into the middle of the circle. All the cupids were staring at her. She did not want to go. She knew she would not be able to beat Harper. She would not even be able to go as high as Sophie.

"Just do your best," Harper said. "And concentrate real hard."

Willa Bean's lower lip trembled. Her knees shook.

And just then, the bell rang.

"All right, cupids!" Miss Twizzle called. "Recess is over! Let's get back in line!"

With a shout, the cupids turned around and followed Miss Twizzle.

"We'll start with you next time we play, Willa Bean!" Harper said. "Don't worry!"

Willa Bean stayed behind a little as Harper raced up ahead. She could feel her breaths coming out of her mouth in little spurts.

It was going to be impossible not to worry. Worrying was one of the things she did best.

Chapter 4

Companionship

Later that night, Willa Bean got ready for bed. First, she put on her yellow night-gown and fuzzy orange slippers. Then she turned on the two night-lights by her bed. She opened her door a little so she could see the light in the hallway. Finally, she went over and tapped on her closet door.

There was no answer.

Willa Bean tapped again, a little harder this time.

Still no answer.

She puckered up her lips and gave a low whistle. "Snooze!" she whispered. "Are you in there?"

A rustling sound came from inside the closet, followed by a short sneeze. *"Oui,"* Snooze answered. *Oui* meant *yes* in French.

Willa Bean swung open her closet door. Usually at this time of the night, Snooze was fluffing his feathers with his beak. Or doing his wing exercises to get ready for his night flight around the world.

Tonight, though, Snooze had his beak tucked under one wing. He squinted as the light from Willa Bean's room came into the closet. Then he sneezed again. It sounded like this: *"Twoot!"*

"Snooze!" Willa Bean said. "You look terrible! What's the matter?"

Snooze blinked. "I hab a code," he said. His voice sounded stuffy.

Willa Bean leaned into the closet a little more. "A *what*?"

"A code," Snooze repeated. "I hab a code."

"Are you speaking in French?" Willa Bean asked. "Because I don't understand a word you're saying."

Snooze ruffled his feathers weakly. He sniffled through his beak, and rubbed one of his big yellow eyes with the tip of his wing. "I hab a COLD," he said. "I'm sick."

"Oh, Snooze!" Willa Bean reached up and cradled her little owl in her arms. "You have a *cold*! That's why your nose is all stuffy! Where did you get a cold from?"

Snooze nestled against Willa Bean's arm. "I hab no idea," he said.

"It's all that flying you do out in the uvinerse," Willa Bean said. "Maybe you got it in Morocco."

"It's pronounced *u-NI-verse*, Willa Bean," Snooze said. "Not *u-VI-nerse*."

"That's what I said." Willa Bean nodded. "Uvinerse."

Snooze sighed. He closed his eyes.

"Do you need any medicine?" Willa Bean asked. "When I get sick, Mama gives me a teaspoon of moonbeam syrup. It tastes yucky, but it always makes me feel better in the morning. Do you want me to get you some moonbeam syrup?"

"I don't think moonbeam syrup is going to work for me," Snooze said. "Dat's just for cupids."

"Well, what do owls take when they get sick?" Willa Bean asked. "You have to take something, or else you won't get better!"

Snooze shook his head. "There isn't any medicine for owls. We just hab to stay quiet and get lots of extra sleep." He closed his eyes again and pulled one wing over his eye. "A little extra companionship helps, too."

"What's companionship?" Willa Bean asked.

"Being with you," Snooze answered. "I don't like being alone when I'm sick. It makes me feel even worse. Being with you makes me feel better. I always feel a little stronger afterward."

Willa Bean patted Snooze's head softly. She smoothed his wing feathers and let him snuggle close against her. Snooze curled his tiny feet under him. He breathed in and out through his stuffy nose.

"Snooze?" Willa Bean said after a moment.

"Hmmm?" Snooze opened one eye.

"Do you like flying up high?"

"I do," Snooze said.

"What about the dark?" Willa Bean asked. "Do you like flying in the dark?"

"I do," Snooze said again. "Very much."

"But isn't it scary?" Willa Bean asked. "Flying up so high? And in the dark?" She shivered just thinking about it.

Snooze ruffled a wing feather. "No. It's quite exciting, actually."

"But what if you fell when you were high up? And how can you see without any lights on? How can you tell where you're *going*?"

"I've never fallen," Snooze said. "That's what my wings are for. They keep me up. And there are plenty of lights out there. What do you think the moon is? And all those stars?"

"But there's lots more dark than stars," Willa Bean said. "And what if one of the stars wasn't working right, and it wasn't bright enough, and you thought you were flying the right way but really you weren't, and you crashed into something or got lost out there in the middle of the uvinerse and no one could ever find you again?" She took a breath. "Then what?"

Snooze blinked. "I'm dizzy all of a sudden," he said.

"But still," Willa Bean said. "What if?"

"Nothing like that has ever happened,"

Snooze said. "To the best of my knowledge, all the stars are working just fine. And they probably will be for quite some time."

Willa Bean thought about the trip Harper had taken last weekend with her father. They had flown all the way around the Milky Way and then home again. It had been super-dark. So dark, Harper said, that she couldn't see her hand in front of her face!

Willa Bean couldn't imagine doing such a thing.

Ever.

Even if every single star in the Milky Way was working perfectly.

"Willa Bean?" Snooze scuttled to the edge of her arm again. "One of the best things about companionship is that it doesn't require very many words. You can just be together. Without talking. Now

I need lots of rest to get better, and you need to go to sleep so you can do well in school tomorrow. So let's not talk anymore tonight, okay? Let's just snuggle."

"Okay," Willa Bean said softly.

Snooze folded his feet back under his chest. "And, Willa Bean?"

"Yeah?"

"Pas de souci," Snooze said.

"Pah duh soo-see?" Willa Bean repeated. "What's that mean?"

"It means don't worry so much!" Snooze answered. "Worrying is for walruses, *ma chérie,* not cupids."

With that, Snooze wiggled in close to Willa Bean's arm. He closed his eyes and went to sleep.

And after a long, long time—and a little bit more worrying—Willa Bean did, too.

Chapter 5

Hairy Ariel

The next morning, Snooze tapped Willa Bean's nose with his beak. *"Bonjour!"* he said.

Willa Bean rubbed her eyes. She wrinkled her nose. "Snooze," she said sleepily. "You need to swish with mouthwash before you breathe on me."

Snooze walked back and forth across Willa Bean's blankets. He ruffled his tail feathers. He blinked his eyes. They were round and bright. "Ah, Willa Bean!" he said. "I feel like a brand-new owl!"

Willa Bean sat up. "No more stuffy nose?"

"Nothing of the sort!" Snooze said. "I told you a good night's sleep and your companionship would make me feel better. And I was right. I feel like I could fly to Jupiter and back!"

Willa Bean gave her little owl a hug. "I'm glad, Snoozer. I hate it when you're sick."

Suddenly, she remembered what today was.

It was Flipday!

Which meant that after school, Harper was coming home with her! To sleep over!

Willa Bean jumped out of bed. She got dressed and brushed her wings. "Good morning, little wings!" she said. "It's a very fantastic day for us! Harper is coming over to spend the night!" Her wings flapped back and forth. They were excited, too.

Willa Bean tried very hard to press her hair down again, but it would not cooperate. *BOING! BOING!* Oh well. Her hair really did have a mind of its own.

Willa Bean slipped on her sandals and went downstairs for breakfast.

"Good morning, little love!" Daddy said. He was sitting at the table with Mama, eating breakfast. "Would you like some help brushing your hair?"

Willa Bean sat down. "I already brushed my hair," she said.

Daddy looked over at Mama.

Mama sighed.

"Well, I'm off," Daddy said. He picked up his quiver in the corner and slung it over his shoulder. Inside the quiver were six golden arrows, glowing in the

morning light. They looked like slivers of a sunbeam.

Daddy leaned over and gave Willa Bean an eyelash kiss. "I'll see you tonight," he said. "Have fun at school."

"Good-bye, Daddy," Willa Bean said. "Good luck!"

She stared at Daddy's arrows as he flew out the door. She was not allowed to touch his golden arrows. Not ever. The same went for Ariel. And for Baby Louie, too, of course. None of them would have golden arrows until they were grown up. Sometimes, though, it was very hard not to touch them. They were so beautiful. And so golden. They were treasure-super-plus.

On the other side of the kitchen, Ariel was opening and shutting the cupboard doors. "Mama, where's the peanut butter?" she asked.

"I think we're out," Mama said.

Ariel turned around. "We're out of *peanut butter*? How are my friends and I supposed to make Snoogy Bars tonight without peanut butter?"

"Don't worry," Mama answered. "Baby Louie and I have to head over to Cloud Seven today for more diapers. I'll get peanut butter while I'm there."

Willa Bean sat up straighter in her chair. "Can you get extra for me, too, Mama?

Harper and I are making our own Snoogy Bars."

"Oh no, you're not," said Ariel. "That's *my* slumber-party project, not yours. You keep out of this kitchen tonight, you little pest."

"You're not the kitchen boss!" Willa Bean said. "Harper and I can make our own Snoogy Bars if we want to. Right, Mama?"

"Why can't you just do it together?" Mama asked. "Everyone can make one gigantic batch of peanut butter Snoogy Bars, and then you can all share them."

"Absolutely not," Ariel said. "I don't want Willa Bean anywhere *near* my Snoogy Bars. Or my friends. And you promised, Mama. You said that if Willa Bean had Harper over, they wouldn't get in our way!"

"I did say that." Mama looked at Willa Bean. "You and Harper will have to think of something else to do, sweetheart."

"That's not fair!" Willa Bean said.

"Too bad." Ariel made a googly face at Willa Bean.

Willa Bean stuck her tongue out at her big sister.

"Whiner," Ariel said.

"Stinker!" Willa Bean yelled.

"Girls," Mama said. "Please. If you can't remember the Cupid Rule, I will cancel everyone's sleepover."

Sometimes Willa Bean wished she had never even heard of the Cupid Rule.

The very best way
To spend your day
Is to try to be kind—
All the time.

It was much too hard to be kind all the time.

Especially to pain-in-the-wing older sisters who thought they were the boss of you.

♥

"Good morning, Willa Bean," Mr. Bibby said a little while later when the cloudbus pulled up. "How are you today?"

"Great, Mr. Bibby!" Willa Bean said. She stared at his bow tie. It was purple with pink stripes. "That's a neat bow tie!" she said.

Mr. Bibby grinned. "This is my lucky bow tie," he said. "Have a seat now. And fasten your cloudbelt."

Harper popped up from their favorite seat in the back. "Willa Bean! Look! I have my wingsack packed! For tonight!"

Willa Bean sat down next to Harper.

She looked at her best friend's wingsack. It was bright orange with strings on the top. The inside was stuffed. There was even something poking out of the top. "What's that?" Willa Bean asked.

"My plastic oar!" Harper yanked open the wingsack and pulled out the oar. "So we can play water boat when we go flying in the dark later!"

Willa Bean swallowed hard. "What else did you pack?"

"Tons of stuff!" Harper took everything out and put it on the seat between them. "Look!" Inside Harper's wingsack, there were:

Yellow shortie pajamas with tiny white bows on the sleeves
Purple slippers
An eyeglass case

A green flashlight

Four packages of Cloudburst Crunch—two for each of them!

Six rubber spiders

A lightning-and-thunder noisemaker—with extra batteries!

One can of lavender mooncream

Harper leaned over and whispered something in Willa Bean's ear. It had to do with the spiders, and the lightning-and-thunder noisemaker, and the lavender mooncream.

Willa Bean began to giggle. Then she began to wiggle. "You thought of everything, Harper! We are going to scare the wings off of Ariel and her friends! I can't wait!"

Chapter 6

The Wigglies

It was hard for Willa Bean to concentrate in school. Her wiggly-jiggly feeling was out of control. It was spilling out of her wings. It was coming out of her fingertips and shooting out of her toes!

Miss Twizzle was teaching the class how to write Nifty Notes. They were a very important part of being a cupid.

"Pay attention, cupids," Miss Twizzle said. "Sometimes on Earth, you will see children who are sad. Most of the time, you will use one of your friendship arrows to make them feel better. But you don't always have to do that. You can leave a Nifty Note instead. Nifty Notes are just one or two words written on a piece of paper. You put them in a secret place for the Earth child to find. They will make him or her feel happy again. All right, let's practice."

Miss Twizzle wrote, "Cheer up!" on the board.

Willa Bean copied it into her notebook with her quill pen. That was a good Nifty Note. She jiggled her leg and wiggled her wings. This was fun.

Next, Miss Twizzle wrote, "You're sweet!"

Willa Bean squiggled in her seat. She copied that Nifty Note into her notebook, too. But it was getting harder and harder to pay attention.

Three more Nifty Notes went into their notebooks.

"Hang on!"

"You rock!"

"Be brave!"

Next, Miss Twizzle asked the class to think up their own Nifty Note. She told them to write it in their notebooks. Willa Bean thought and thought. She nibbled on the end of her quill pen. Finally, she wrote something down.

"Who would like to put their Nifty Note on the board?" Miss Twizzle asked.

Willa Bean raised her hand. So did Vivi.

"All right, Willa Bean," Miss Twizzle said. "You can go first."

Willa Bean jumped out of her chair. She ran through the space between the desks. She almost tripped over Pedro's foot.

"Hey!" said Pedro. "That was my foot!"

"Sorry!" Willa Bean whispered. "My feet are a little wiggly today."

Willa Bean stood in front of the board. Then she wrote out her Nifty Note. It said, "Let's fly!"

She turned around and looked at Miss Twizzle. She was very proud of herself. She knew that any Earth child would love to go flying with her.

But Miss Twizzle looked worried. She scratched her nose and shook her head. "No, Willa Bean," she said. "Remember when we talked about this? People on Earth aren't like us. They don't have wings. They can't fly."

"Oh." Willa Bean could feel her cheeks get hot. She had forgotten that lesson. "Well, how do they get around, then?" she asked.

Miss Twizzle looked out at the class. "Can anyone remind Willa Bean how Earth people get around?"

A lot of hands went up. Vivi waved hers back and forth like a flag. Pedro stood up out of his seat. Even Harper leaned forward. "Oh, oh!" she said. "Pick me, Miss Twizzle! Pick me!"

"All right, Harper," Miss Twizzle said. "Tell Willa Bean how Earth people get around since they don't have wings."

"They walk and run like us," Harper said. "But when they want to get some-where super-fast, they have to go in a plane. Planes have wings, but not like ours. They're fake."

"Thank you, Harper." Miss Twizzle looked at Willa Bean. "Now, can you think of something else you might say in your Nifty Note?"

Willa Bean stared at her toes. She wig-gled them inside her sandals. Then she looked up. "How about 'Be wiggly'?" she asked.

Miss Twizzle wrinkled her forehead. "'Be wiggly'?" she repeated.

"Yeah!" Willa Bean jumped up and down. She shook her wings back and forth. "Like this! So they can have fun! And be happy!"

Miss Twizzle sighed. "Well, I'm not sure if they would understand what you have in mind, exactly. But you can write that down for now."

Willa Bean turned back around. She wrote the words carefully on the blackboard. "Be wiggly!" She thought it was a wonderful Nifty Note.

Afterward, as everyone lined up for recess, Miss Twizzle came over to Willa Bean.

"Willa Bean," Miss Twizzle whispered. "Do you by any chance have ants in your pants today?"

Willa Bean giggled. "No, Miss Twizzle. I'm just excited. I'm having my first-ever sleepover at my house tonight! With Harper! And I'm full of the wigglies just thinking about it!"

"Oh." Miss Twizzle smiled. "Well, now I understand. But the final bell is a little ways off, Willa Bean. You need to try to stay calm until then. Do you think you can do that?"

"Well," Willa Bean said, "I will try my hardest."

Chapter 7

Tip-Top Again!

Willa Bean did try her hardest. In fact, she tried so hard to keep her wigglies under control that she completely forgot about the Tip-Top game at recess.

"You're up, Willa Bean!" Pedro said as everyone went outside. "You're the last one from yesterday! Let's see how high you can get!"

The cupids formed a circle around Willa Bean.

"Come on, Willa Bean!" Harper yelled.

"I bet you can beat me! I bet you can go even higher!"

"Start off super-fast," Raymond said. He pulled his little red hat down around his ears. "That way, you won't wobble."

Willa Bean stared at Raymond's red hat. Her hands had already started to shake. Should she ask him if she could borrow it? She looked up. She tried to see the bottom of the baby cloud above her. But it was too high. There was nothing up there except sky. And then more sky.

"Go, Willa Bean!" said Lola. "You can do it!"

Willa Bean rubbed one of her eyes.

She straightened her back.

She raised her arms over her head and pressed her fingertips together.

She would have to go higher than she had ever gone in her whole entire life. And what if her wings got too tired? What if they just pooped out and stopped working altogether? And then she fell? Who would catch her?

She dropped her arms. "I don't feel like it," she said.

The cupids stared at her.

"Why not?" Harper asked finally.

Willa Bean shrugged. She walked over and sat down on one of the orange swings. "I just changed my mind," she said. "I don't want to play this game."

"But you *have* to play!" Raymond insisted. "It's Tip-Top! Everyone gets a turn!"

"Well, I give my turn to someone else,"

Willa Bean said. "'Cause I don't want it."

Raymond and Pedro looked at each other. "That's not how we play," Pedro said. "Those aren't the rules."

Willa Bean bit her lip. She stared at her sandals.

"*I* know what's wrong," Vivi said. She pushed her way to the front of the cupid group. "Willa Bean's *scared* to go up high. That's why she doesn't want to play. She's a big scaredy-star!"

Willa Bean jumped out of her swing. "Am not!" she said.

"Yes, you are," Vivi said. "You're just a big baby, Willa Bean Skylight, and you know it!"

"And you're the meanest cupid in the whole uvinerse!" Willa Bean shouted back.

"Am not!" Vivi hollered.

"Are too!" Willa Bean hollered back.

"Cupids!" Miss Twizzle came running over. She looked annoyed. "What are you two fighting about now?"

"Willa Bean said that Vivi was the meanest cupid in the whole universe," Raymond said.

"But that's just because Vivi called Willa Bean a scaredy-star," Harper offered. "Which was not very nice at all."

"Neither of those things are very nice," Miss Twizzle said. She looked at Vivi. Then she looked at Willa Bean. "And I am getting tired of having to step between the two of you every day. If you can't remember the Cupid Rule in my classroom, I am going to have to send both of you to the principal. Is that understood?"

Vivi wrinkled her nose. She poked at the ground with her shoe and nodded her head.

Willa Bean squeezed her eyes shut tight. She hated to disappoint Miss Twizzle. She nodded her head, too. "Yes, Miss Twizzle," she whispered.

"All right, then," Miss Twizzle said. "Now, it sounds as if this game is causing too many hurt feelings. So I want all of you to play something else."

"I know!" Pedro yelled. "Let's play Wingtag! I'm it!"

Willa Bean opened her eyes. She smiled at her teacher.

Miss Twizzle always knew just what to say.

She was the best teacher in the whole entire world. Maybe even in the whole entire uvinerse.

Chapter 8

The Plan

"Good-bye, Mr. Bibby!" Willa Bean and Harper yelled. They were getting off the cloudbus at their cloudstop.

"Just a minute, you two." Mr. Bibby sat up in his seat. He straightened his purple-and-pink bow tie.

Willa Bean stopped walking. So did Harper.

Mr. Bibby looked at them carefully. "Do either of you happen to know anything about a Snoogy Bar mess in the backseat?" he asked.

Willa Bean looked at Harper.

Harper looked back at Willa Bean.

"Snoogy Bar?" Willa Bean said. "What Snoogy Bar?"

Mr. Bibby gave Willa Bean a stern look. "I know best friends stick together," he said. "But they still have to tell the truth. Even when it's about each other."

Harper sighed. "It was me, Mr. Bibby. I got blueberry goo all over my hands, and I didn't have a tissue, so I wiped it on the seat." She blinked her big eyes. "I'm sorry."

"Well, I cleaned it up this time," Mr. Bibby said. "But if it happens again, you will have to stay and clean it yourself."

Harper nodded. "I won't do it again," she said. "I promise."

"All right, then." Mr. Bibby smiled at

the girls. "Go ahead now. Have a good weekend."

"We're having a sleepover!" Willa Bean said.

"Is that so?" Mr. Bibby asked. "What fun! I want to hear all about it on Moon-day!"

"Okay, Mr. Bibby!" said Harper. "See you later!"

And with a chug and two bursts, the cloudbus took off.

"Hello, Harper!" Mama said as the girls got home. "It's so nice to see you again!" She was sitting on the kitchen floor, rolling a red rubber star-bubble ball to Baby Louie. It was his favorite toy.

Harper put her wingsack on the kitchen table. She got down on the floor next to Baby Louie. "Hi, Mrs. Skylight," she said.

"I can't wait to sleep over. Thanks for inviting me."

"You're most welcome," said Mama.

Willa Bean sat next to Harper. They played ball with Baby Louie for a few minutes. But it got pretty boring. Especially since Baby Louie couldn't throw. Or catch. Plus, whenever he got the ball, he drooled all over it.

It made a slobbery, disgusting mess.

"C'mon, Harper," Willa Bean said. "Let's go up to my room."

"Some of Ariel's friends are here already," Mama said. "Make sure you don't get in their way up there. I don't want to hear any bickering!"

"Okay, Mama!" Willa Bean said. But she stopped when she came to Ariel's door. She pressed her ear against it. So did Harper. They could hear shrieks and giggles inside. There was a yell. Then more shrieks.

Harper looked at Willa Bean. "What are they *doing* in there?" she asked.

Willa Bean shrugged. "Maybe a pillow fight?"

Suddenly, Ariel's door flew open. "Are you out here snooping on us?" Ariel's blond hair was a mess. Her wings were mussed and wrinkly. The feathers on top

were bent over. Behind her, three other
cupids poked their heads out. They were a
mess, too.

Willa Bean took a step back. So did Harper. Then Willa Bean started to laugh. She couldn't help it. Her big sister looked so funny with her hair all over the place, and her wings bent and wrinkly.

"What are you laughing at?" Ariel yelled.

"Your hair!" Willa Bean giggled. "And your wings! You look so silly!"

"You get out of here, Willa Bean!" Ariel said. "And if I find you snooping out here again, I'll go down and tell Mama!" She leaned in close. "And then Mama will make Harper leave!"

Harper tugged on Willa Bean's arm. "C'mon, Willa Bean," she said. "Let's go in your room."

Ariel slammed her door.

Willa Bean and Harper went inside Willa Bean's room.

They sat down on the floor. Harper emptied her wingsack. They spread out everything they were going to need on the rug:

One green flashlight
Six rubber spiders
One lightning-and-thunder noisemaker
One can of lavender mooncream

Next, Harper and Willa Bean made their plan.

They laughed and giggled. They covered their mouths so that no one could hear.

It was a perfect plan.

It was incredibly exciting.

And it was going to scare the woolly-bully-wing-wang out of Ariel and her friends!

Chapter 9

Trouble!

After dinner, Willa Bean and Harper snuck upstairs. Mama and Daddy were in the den, playing with Baby Louie. Ariel and her friends were in the kitchen, making a super batch of peanut butter Snoogy Bars. Willa Bean and Harper had the whole upstairs to themselves. It was the perfect time to start their plan.

They crept into Ariel's room. They squirted gobs of mooncream under Ariel's pillow. They hid two rubber spiders in

her bed. Willa Bean was about to put the lightning-and-thunder noisemaker behind the door when she stopped.

"Oh!" she gasped.

Harper whirled around. She had two more rubber spiders in her hand. "What's wrong?" she whispered.

Willa Bean pointed behind Ariel's door. "Look!" she said.

Harper stared at the golden arrow lying on the floor. "Is that one of your dad's arrows?" she whispered.

Willa Bean nodded. "Ariel must've snuck it up here after Daddy got home," she said. "I betcha they're all going to sneak off to Cloud Two later, so Ariel can try to use it in her bow. She just wants to show off to all her friends!"

"What if one of Ariel's friends touches it?" Harper asked. "Won't it be ruined?"

Willa Bean nodded. "Daddy won't ever be able to use it again if one of Ariel's friends touches it. Golden arrows can only be touched by family! Else they won't work!"

"Wizzle-dizzle-doodad!" Harper said. "Ariel's gonna get into some serious trouble if your dad finds out!"

"Let's get out of here," Willa Bean said. "I don't want Daddy to think we had anything to do with *this*!"

Willa Bean and Harper crept back into Willa Bean's room. They sat on her bed and played two games of Go Planet. Harper won the first game, and Willa Bean won the second. Snooze sat on top of Willa Bean's pillow and watched them play.

Next, they sorted through their treasures. Willa Bean brought out her three copper coins, a black-and-white-striped feather, and two silver rings. Harper had found a white marble, three hot-pink feathers, and an oval bead. The two cupids cleaned each treasure with a soft cloth. Then they dropped them in Willa Bean's leather pouch. Tomorrow, they would fly to Cloud Five and put everything in their treasure chest.

After they were done with the treasure, they built a fort out of Willa Bean's blankets. Snooze pretended to be the guard. He marched up and down outside the fort. "Hup, two, three, four," he said, keeping his wings straight. "Hup! Hup!"

"You're a very good fort guard," Willa Bean said.

"Thank you," said Snooze. "I aim to please." He settled himself on the window ledge and looked back at Willa Bean and Harper. "Well, it's time for me to be off," he said.

"Where are you going tonight?" Willa Bean asked.

"I have some unfinished business in Morocco," Snooze said. "There are a few family members I still want to visit. I'll see you in the morning, *chéries*." And with a wiggle of his tail and three flaps of his wings, he sailed off into the night sky.

It was very dark outside when Ariel and her friends finally came back upstairs. Willa Bean and Harper ran to Ariel's door and listened. But there were no screams about spiders. No yelling about lavender mooncream. And no jumping up and down under the lightning-and-thunder noisemaker. Instead, they heard Ariel's window open.

Willa Bean couldn't stand it anymore. She pushed open Ariel's door a tiny crack. Then she peeked inside. One by one, the older cupids flew out the window and disappeared into the black night. Ariel was in the very front, with Daddy's golden arrow in her hand. Ding, her pet dragonfly, flew next to her.

"Let's go!" Harper whispered. She yanked on Willa Bean's sleeve. "We can follow them!"

But Willa Bean took a step away from the dark window. And then another. "No way," she said. "It's too cold out there."

"You won't even feel the cold when you're flying!" Harper said. She pulled on Willa Bean's sleeve again. "Come on! It'll be fun! And it's super-dark, so we can just hide under the cloud! They won't even see us!"

Willa Bean looked out the window. She could see the moon. It was shaped like a crescent. It looked like a tiny white thumbnail. Around it, the sky was an inky black. She shook her head. "Let's make our Snoogy Bars," she said. "Mama bought some chocolate."

Harper's shoulders sagged. "Who wants

to eat *now*?" she asked. "This is exciting! This will be an adventure!"

"I don't feel like it," Willa Bean said.

"Oh please, Willa Bean!" Harper said. "Pleasepleasepleaseplease*please*?"

"I can't," Willa Bean said. "I think I'm coming down with a cold. Maybe the same one Snooze got. From Morocco. It could be a spicy cold. Those are very hard to get better from."

"Oh, *Willa Bean*." Harper slumped down on the floor. "You're no fun."

Willa Bean didn't like it when her best friend said things like that. She *was* fun! But how could she tell Harper—who had won the whole entire game of Tip-Top at school—that she was afraid? That following Ariel meant having to do two of the things that scared her the most? Flying high. In the dark. At the same time!

"I am *too* fun," Willa Bean said quietly. "I just don't want to do this."

"Fine." Harper stuck her legs out straight in front of her. She looked up at the ceiling and crossed her arms across her chest. "We can just stay here, then."

Willa Bean sat down next to her best friend. "Staying here's okay, isn't it?" she asked.

Harper nodded.

But Willa Bean knew it didn't mean yes.

Chapter 10

Be Brave, Willa Bean!

A little while later, Harper and Willa Bean were in the middle of another round of Go Planet. Suddenly, a loud noise sounded at Willa Bean's window. Harper jumped. So did Willa Bean. "Toodle-doodle-wing-wang!" Harper yelled. "Look!"

All three of Ariel's friends were trying to get into Willa Bean's room. So was Ding. Ariel's friends were carrying her in their arms. Ding was flying very close to Ariel's left ear. Ariel was crying.

"What happened?" Willa Bean asked.

"I fell!" Ariel clutched Willa Bean's hand. "I hurt my wing, and I can't fly. It hurts too much. And I . . ." Ariel cried harder. "I took Daddy's golden arrow, Willa Bean. I just wanted to try it. One time! But after I got hurt, I accidentally left it on Cloud Two. You have to go back and get it for me! Please, Willa Bean!"

Willa Bean's face turned white. "I can't," she said.

"You have to!" Ariel said. "No one else is allowed to touch it! You know that! Please go get Daddy's arrow so I can put it back. And then we can all do something together. In my room."

Willa Bean looked out the window again.

Cloud Two was all the way on the other side of Nimbus. It was up very high. In fact, of all of Nimbus's nine clouds, it was the highest.

She stuck her hand out the window. It was so dark that she could barely see it in front of her.

There was no way she could do it.

No way, nohow.

Nope, nope-ity, nope, nope, nope.

Her inside crying feeling was starting to bubble up. She could feel her nose getting wrinkly. Her eyes were starting to burn.

She swallowed hard and stamped her foot. She was not going to cry in front of Harper. Or Ariel and all her friends!

"Willa Bean." Ariel sniffed. "Please. You're going to have to hurry. Mama and Daddy will be coming upstairs soon. You have to get that arrow for me."

Willa Bean bit her lip. Why couldn't she have a magic red hat, like Raymond had? Or a lucky bow tie, like Mr. Bibby's? She wasn't even tall, like Hannah. She was tiny. After Sophie, she was the shortest cupid in Class A! There was nothing about her that would make her brave. Nothing at all.

"I'll go with you," Harper said. "The whole way, Willa Bean." Harper leaned in close, so that Ariel couldn't hear. "And I'll hold your hand, too, if you want."

Just then, Snooze appeared. He settled

down on the ledge of Willa Bean's window and closed his wings.

"Snooze!" Willa Bean said. "What are you doing here? I thought you left for Morocco."

"I did," Snooze said. "But on my way down, I saw Ariel's friends flying back here. I thought there might be trouble, so I turned around again." He raised an eyebrow at Ariel. "And it looks like I was right."

Ariel looked at the floor. "It was an accident," she said.

"Come on," Snooze said. "I'll go with you, too, Willa Bean. We don't have much time. And we have to get that arrow."

Willa Bean took a deep breath. She thought about what Snooze had said to her the night before. About companionship. He'd said it made him feel better when he was sick. That it even made him feel stronger after a while.

Maybe, just maybe, Harper and Snooze's companionship would do the same thing for her now. Maybe she would start off scared, the way Snooze had started off sick, and then it would change. She would get stronger. Braver. Because she was with them.

"Okay." Willa Bean's voice was very trembly. Her fingers shook. Her knees felt a little wobbly. "Let's go," she said.

Ariel and her friends watched as Willa Bean stood in her window. Snooze settled in on Willa Bean's shoulder. "I'm right here," he whispered. *"Courage,* Willa Bean!"* That meant *Be brave!* in French.

Harper stood on the other side of Willa Bean. She took her best friend's hand. "You ready?" she asked.

Willa Bean shook her head from side to side. "No," she whispered.

"Go anyway!" Snooze said. "One, two, three!"

The two cupids pushed themselves off the window ledge. They flapped their wings and soared into the darkness. The very dark darkness. Willa Bean squeezed her eyes shut. Her cheeks were cold. Her hair whooshed around her face. She felt like crying.

But Snooze flew up ahead and then turned around. "Look at me, Willa Bean!" he said. "You're doing it! You're flying up high! The highest you've ever been! And in the dark!"

Slowly, Willa Bean opened one eye. And then the other. Snooze was right there, flying in front of her. He was flapping his brown wings and talking with his

little yellow beak. She could see him!

Next to her, Harper squeezed her hand. Willa Bean looked over. Harper's hair was streaming behind her. Her white wings glowed in the dark. She could see Harper, too!

"Look up ahead," Snooze called. "Do you see the North Star? Can you see how

bright it is? It will give us lots of light—the
whole way!"

Willa Bean looked at the North Star. It
was as big as a pumpkin. It pulsed a soft
white color. It was like a night-light in the
heavens. Maybe two night-lights.

"And look at all the other stars!" Harper
said. "There's a million of them!"

Willa Bean looked around. Harper was right. There were a million other stars out, besides the North Star. Each one burned bright. Each one lit up the darkness a little bit. It was not so dark here, after all.

Willa Bean squeezed Harper's hand tightly when they came close to the top of Cloud Two. It was very high up. Extremely high up. But somehow, with Snooze and Harper there, it did not seem so terrible. It did not seem so scary.

Daddy's golden arrow was off to one side. It was lying next to the cloudbridge. Willa Bean picked it up carefully. It was heavy! She tucked it inside the waistband of her dress. She tightened the belt so that it would not slide out.

And then, with Harper and Snooze on either side of her, Willa Bean flew back home.

Up high.

And in the dark.

Much later, after Daddy's arrow had been put back in his quiver and Ariel's wing had been fixed and bandaged, Willa Bean heard a knock on her door.

"Willa Bean?" It was Ariel. "Can I come in?"

Willa Bean looked at Harper. Her best friend was dressed up as a moonqueen. She had Willa Bean's blue comforter over her head, with a crown on top of it. Mama's big gold shoes were on her feet. There was a sparkly wand in her hand. "What do you think, Queen Harper?" Willa Bean asked. "Can Ariel come in?"

"Ah, yes," Queen Harper said. "Enter, Ariel!"

Ariel came into the room. She did not

look at Harper. Instead, she sat down on Willa Bean's bed. "Willa Bean," she said, "I'm so sorry for the way I acted before. For calling you a baby and a whiner, and all that. And for saying you couldn't hang out with us."

"You were pretty mean," Willa Bean agreed.

"You had no reason to help me," Ariel went on. "But you did anyway. And I just want you to know that it means a lot to me. You're a great little sister, Willa Bean."

Ariel hugged Willa Bean tight.

Willa Bean hugged her back.

Behind them, Harper raised her sparkly wand. "Ah, yes!" she said. "Queen Harper can fix anything!"

"You didn't fix this, you little squirt," Ariel said. "Willa Bean did."

There was another knock on the door. It was Mama. "I hate to bring bad news," she said, looking at everyone. "But it's time for bed." She raised an eyebrow at Ariel. "You included, Ariel."

Ariel stood up. "Okay, Mama. Good night, Willa Bean."

"Good night, Ariel," Willa Bean said.

"Oh, I like the sound of *that*," Mama said. "I knew you two would figure a way to work things out."

Willa Bean and Harper got into their pajamas. They brushed their teeth, and gargled with mouthwash, and spit everything into the sink. Willa Bean turned on her night-lights and slid under the covers. Harper was right next to her. Mama gave them both an eyelash kiss good night.

"Mama?" Willa Bean said as she left the room. "Don't forget to leave the door open a little."

"Don't worry," Mama said, keeping the door open a crack. "I won't forget."

Harper sat up. "Actually," she said,

"would it be okay if you opened it all the way?"

"Of course." Mama left the door open wide and blew another kiss into the room.

Willa Bean stared at Harper.

Harper looked up at the ceiling.

"Harper?" Willa Bean said finally.

"Yes?"

"*You're* not afraid of the dark, are you?"

"No." Harper rolled over and looked at Willa Bean. "But I've never slept over at anyone's house before. And I'm just a little bit nervous." Harper nibbled on one of her fingernails. "You don't think I'm a baby, do you?"

Willa Bean thought about what Mr. Bibby had said on the bus. About how best friends needed to stick together *and* tell the truth. "I think everything's a little bit easier with companionship," she said.

"You mean like being together?" Harper asked.

"Yes!" Willa Bean hooked her arm through Harper's. "Like being together."

"I would definitely be more scared if you weren't here," Harper said. "Being with you makes it easy."

Willa Bean smiled. Underneath the covers, she opened her hand a bit. Inside was a tiny piece of cloud that she had grabbed from Cloud Two. It was purple and fluffy and just starting to melt.

It was the most beautiful thing she had ever seen.

More
Little Wings

Fall in love with the pluckiest cupid in the clouds—

Willa Bean Skylight!

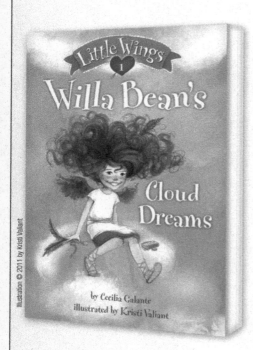

Most cupids have soft, straight hair, rosy cheeks, and silky white wings. Not Willa Bean! She has crazy curls, a million-bajillion freckles, and bright purple wings with silver tips. And lately those bright purple wings have been giving Willa Bean an awful lot of problems. They won't fly! Cupid Academy is starting soon, and what if she's the only cloud-bound cupid there? Nope, nope, nope-ity, nope. Willa Bean just has to make her wings behave!

RANDOM HOUSE
CHILDREN'S BOOKS

SteppingStonesBooks.com